Sheila Lane a

Travellers' Tales
Stories from Grimm

CAMBRIDGE UNIVERSITY PRESS
Cambridge
London   New York   New Rochelle
Melbourne   Sydney

Travellers' Tales

This story takes place in the town of Cassel, in Germany, where Jacob and Wilhelm Grimm, the famous collectors of tales, spent the early part of their lives.

The book begins with Jacob and Wilhelm listening to stories told by the local people. The brothers are writing down these tales, not because they are 'pretty stories', but because they are an important part of the history of their country.

In this book, as each tale is told by one of the story-tellers, it comes to life as a play. The characters who take part in the plays are the **Playmakers**. The story-tellers, the listeners and the two Grimm brothers, are the **Playwatchers**.

Contents

PLAYWATCHERS

People of Cassel

JACOB GRIMM
WILHELM GRIMM ⎤ who are collecting stories

THE ARTIST who tells the first story
THE OLD SOLDIER who tells the second story
THE EGG-WIFE who tells the third story

Other people of the town

THE ARTIST *sets up his easel in the town square and begins to paint.*
TOWNSPEOPLE *wander in and watch him at work. Enter* JACOB *and*
WILHELM GRIMM, *each carrying a pile of notebooks and paper.*

JACOB   More and more stories, Wilhelm!

WILHELM   Think of the treasure we hold in our arms, Jacob.
Pure gold!

JACOB   (*laughing*) And as heavy as gold, too! (*They put the
notebooks on a bench at the side of the arena and sit
down.*)

WILHELM   (*thoughtfully*) Jacob! Perhaps we should make one
great book of all these tales. (*excitedly*) It would be
a great book!

JACOB   I'm not so sure. (*thoughtfully*) One great book...
that might destroy the magic – and then all would
be lost.

WILHELM   But... if people stop telling their tales and they
are not written down, the tales will be lost – for
ever!

JACOB   That's true...and people do CHANGE their stories. (*tapping paper*) We must be sure that we have the true tales here.

WILHELM   (*waving towards artist*) I think we can be sure today, brother. That's the painter fellow they told us about in Hesse.

JACOB   (*getting up*) So it is! Let's hear what he has to say.

WILHELM   I've heard he tells a story well.

(JACOB *and* WILHELM *walk over to join the others, carrying their notebooks. Everyone settles down to listen to the* ARTIST *as he puts down his brush.*)

ARTIST   (*smiling*) Is it a tale you're waiting for?

LISTENERS   We are! We are!

ARTIST   (*pointing to easel*)
A story in paint on my canvas you see,
But now for the words...so listen to me.
Of the proud Leonora a tale I'll unfold,
A princess of beauty, but haughty and cold.
Whoever came near her,
nobody pleased her!
Try as they would,
plead as they would,
NOBODY pleased her!

Here begins The story of the Proud Princess.

The Story of The Proud Princess

Playmakers

PRINCESS LEONORA
KING
QUEEN
MARSHAL of the Court

LORD HAMBURG
LORD FRANKFURT
THE EARL OF ROOS
THE DUKE OF HANOVER } suitors of the Princess Leonora
THE DUKE OF GRENA
PRINCE ALEXANDER

LORD CHAMBERLAIN
PAGE
Other servants } at Prince Alexander's castle
Guests

HANS
HERMAN } friends of Prince Alexander
SKULD

The Story of The Proud Princess

LORD HAMBURG *and* LORD FRANKFURT *come into the arena from different directions.*

HAMBURG Ah! Frankie, my dear fellow! How good to see you!

FRANKFURT (*holding out both arms*) Ham! My old friend!

HAMBURG Tell me, Frankie, do you fancy your chances with this Princess Leonora?

FRANKFURT I fancy her money, Ham! (*rubbing hands together*) I fancy her money!

HAMBURG Well, well! I always thought you favoured Miranda, the Lord Chamberlain's pretty daughter.

FRANKFURT I did...I did...but that's a sad story.

HAMBURG (*laughing and digging Frankfurt in the ribs*) Ha-ha! So Miranda wouldn't have you! And she has such a pretty face.

FRANKFURT A pretty face...yes! But money...no! Miranda has no money, old friend. So...(*He opens his hands.*)

HAMBURG Ho-ho! So Miranda's face is her fortune, and you're broke – as usual.

FRANKFURT (*showing pocket linings*) I'm broke all right! I'm STONY BROKE! (*looks round*) Who's this coming?

(THE EARL OF ROOS *comes in.*)

ROOS (*waving arm*) Hallo there, Ham! Good-day to you, Frankie!

HAMBURG (*admiringly*) You do look a fine fellow today, Roos!

FRANKFURT	All in red! I must say, you look rather...dangerous!
ROOS	Dangerous! Dangerous! Aha! They do say that the dear Leonora is a very DANGEROUS lady. (*He rubs his hands together.*)
HAMBURG	(*making a face*) I'm terrified of her!
FRANKFURT	Me too! But when I start trembling (*shaking*) I think of her money!
ROOS	I wish you two fellows the best of luck, of course, (*twirling round on heel*) but I'm hoping to stand out in the crowd! Ha! (*waving hand*) Here come some more...hopefuls.
	(*Enter the* MARSHAL *of the Court,* THE DUKE OF HANOVER *and* THE DUKE OF GRENA.)
MARSHAL	(*bowing*) His Grace the Duke of Hanover and (*bowing*) His Grace the Duke of Grena. (*He goes out.*)
HANOVER	(*to Hamburg*) Be kind enough to fetch me a chair, there's a good fellow!
GRENA	(*to Frankfurt*) And some refreshments, my man.
HAMBURG	I'd better introduce myself. I'm LORD Hamburg and not at your service. (*waving hand towards Frankfurt*) And this is my friend, LORD Frankfurt.
HANOVER	LORDS! Oh! I do beg your pardon.
GRENA	(*to Frankfurt*) A thousand pardons! I thought you were the butler! (*to Hanover*) It must be that red fellow, then. (*to Roos*) Don't just stand there, man. Go and get us something to eat...and drink.
ROOS	Sorry, old chap! I'm here to try my luck too.
GRENA	Are we to understand that you three are all suitors for the hand of the lovely Leonora?

10

ALL THREE	We are!
	(*Enter the* MARSHAL *of the Court, followed by* PRINCE ALEXANDER, *an important-looking bearded gentleman.*)
MARSHAL	(*bowing low*) This way, your Royal Highness. (*He hurries out.*)
ALL SUITORS	Royal Highness! (*all bow*) Your Royal Highness!
HAMBURG	I don't think I know you, my dear fellow. May I introduce myself? I'm Lord Hamburg, and this (*waving towards Frankfurt*) is Lord Frankfurt, and (*waving towards Roos*) this bright fellow here is the Earl of Roos.
ALEXANDER	Charmed, I'm sure.
GRENA	(*importantly*) I'm the DUKE of Grena, (*waving hand*) and this is another DUKE...the Duke of Hanover.
ROOS	(*to Alexander*) Oh well! The more the merrier, I suppose. Come and join the queue!
	(MARSHAL *comes in, carrying a chair. He moves towards Alexander.*)
MARSHAL	A chair for your Royal Highness.
HAMBURG	Look here, Marshal. I was here first. Why is he getting a chair instead of me?
MARSHAL	(*putting down chair*) Last come, first served, that's what they say. (*bowing to Alexander*) Sit here, your Highness.
FRANKFURT	I hope you're not letting him go in first.
MARSHAL	Nobody's going IN! The Royal Family are all coming OUT! And they're coming out NOW! (*muttering*) And I hope this will be the end of it...the end of that Princess Leonora for a bit, anyway.

11

(The two DUKES, *the two* LORDS *and the* EARL *stand in a row as the* ROYAL PARTY *comes in to the centre of the arena.)*

HANOVER   *(sighing)* At last...the lovely Leonora!

GRENA   She is more beautiful than words can tell.

HAMBURG   Mmm. *(doubtfully)* Just look at her face. *(to Frankfurt)* what do you think of her, Frankie?

FRANKFURT   What do I think of her? It's what she thinks of ME that matters.

ROOS   We shall soon find out!

KING   *(to Leonora)* I'm sick and tired of your ways, Leonora. I've made up my mind. It's NOW or NEVER!

LEONORA   *(laughing and pointing to Suitors)* Which one is NEVER? *(She runs along line and taps each one in turn.)* I'll tell you! Never! Never! Never! Never! Never! Never!

QUEEN   *(anxiously)* Oh, Leonora, don't do that!

KING   *(angrily pulling Leonora back)* I've told you, my girl. You've got to pick a husband now, and you'll find it's no laughing matter if you pick the wrong one.

QUEEN   Do be a good girl, Leonora. Your father has quite made up his mind.

LEONORA   Well, I haven't! Anyway, father never makes up his mind about anything. Why, only the other day...

KING   *(furiously)* You watch your tongue, my girl, or no-one will agree to marry YOU.

LEONORA   What do I care!

QUEEN   *(wringing hands)* Oh, Leonora!

KING   You'll be made to care, my girl, if you don't mend your ways. Marshal! Let's begin.

MARSHAL	Gentlemen! (*looking at Alexander*) Be so good as to stand up when I call your names.
SUITORS	(*except Alexander*) We are standing up.
MARSHAL	Well, you others can stand forward. FIRST, in order of rank, His Royal Highness, the Prince Alexander.

(ALEXANDER *stands up and bows. The others make faces.*)

KING	We are honoured indeed.
QUEEN	(*to Leonora*) Just think, my dear. A prince!
LEONORA	(*walking up to Alexander*) Just look at his beard! (*pulling beard*) Ugh! It's prickly! Hallo... PRICKLY BEARD! (*turning away*) No thank you! I can see he's much too vain anyway.

(ALL SUITORS, *except Alexander, laugh and titter.*)

MARSHAL	(*raising eyes to heaven*) Here we go again! (*loudly*) His Grace, the Duke of Hanover!

(HANOVER *steps forward and smiles graciously.*)

KING	He's a GRAND DUKE, Leonora.
LEONORA	(*running up to him*) And he's a GRAND size. (*running round him*) Phew! I'm quite worn out. No! He's much too fat... just like a dumpling. (*to King*) You can put him in a stew!
MARSHAL	(*quietly*) Put her in a stew! (*loudly*) His Grace, the Duke of Grena!

(GRENA *steps forward and puts out a hand.*)

KING	This is your last chance to have a Duke, Leonora.
LEONORA	I wouldn't want him if he were the last man in the world. What a bean-pole! (*pointing to Grena's head*) Long and thin has little in! That's what they say!

MARSHAL	(*sighing*) It's the same every time! Oh well! Now for the Lords! (*loudly*) The Lord Hamburg!
	(HAMBURG *stands forward and looks straight ahead.*)
KING	You could do worse than have Lord Hamburg, Leonora.
PRINCESS	(*in amazement*) I don't believe it! He's just like a TUB! Short and thick...is never quick! (*She laughs unkindly.*) No, thank you!
MARSHAL	(*aside*) I know what I'd do to her if she were my daughter. (*loudly*) The Lord Frankfurt!
	(FRANKFURT *steps forward looking anxious.*)
KING	(*loudly*) Now, Leonora...
LEONORA	(*interrupting*) Frankfurt! I just can't believe it! (*roaring with laughter*) Hamburger and Frankfurter. SAUSAGES! He's as pale as a ghost, too. I do believe he's frightened of me! (*She runs forward and snaps her fingers in Frankfurt's face.*) I shall call you...WHITEWASH!
MARSHAL	(*aside*) The last one...not long now! (*loudly*) The Earl of...(*to Roos*) Sorry! I've forgotten your name.
ROOS	(*hisses*) ROO – SSS! (*He steps forward.*)
LEONORA	ROOSTER! (*She titters behind her hand.*)
KING	Hold your tongue, Leonora! (*to all*) He's an Earl.
QUEEN	Oh well, an Earl's better than nothing, I suppose.
LEONORA	Look at him! He's as red as a rooster.
KING	Well, you'll have to marry him. That is...if he'll have you.
ROOS	(*rushing forward*) He'll have you...I mean, I'll have you...I mean, I'll have her.
LEONORA	(*stamping foot*) You won't! You won't have me!

14

ROOS   Then who is she going to marry?

SUITORS   WHO IS SHE GOING TO MARRY?

KING   (*with great meaning*) Leonora is going to marry THE VERY NEXT MAN WHO COMES TO THE PALACE GATE.

(ALEXANDER *walks out unnoticed.*)

QUEEN   (*bursting into tears*) No! Oh no!

MARSHAL   (*to Suitors*) Gentlemen! This way.

(SUITORS *follow* MARSHAL *out, grumbling.*)

ARTIST   Now Prince Alexander soon thought of a plan,
And with his good friends to the palace gate ran.
(*He pauses, then points to the Royal group.*)
Inside the Palace the King looked red,
But proud Leonora just tossed her head.
Try as the Queen did,
plead as the Queen did,
the King wouldn't heed her.

QUEEN   (*weeping*) Oh, Leonora! What are we going to do with you?

KING   (*to Queen*) I've told you what I'm going to do with her. She's turned down the Suitors, so...I'm going to give her hand in marriage to the VERY NEXT MAN who comes to the palace gates.

LEONORA   (*tossing head*) I don't care. I don't want to stop here anyway. I'm bored to tears with both of you!

QUEEN   (*sobbing noisily*) Oh, Leonora! How can you speak like that. Oh dear! Oh dear!

(MARSHAL *hurries in with a broad smile on his face.*)

MARSHAL   (*bowing low*) Your Majesty! Your Majesties! There's a...a...MAN...at the palace gate.

KING   (*eagerly*) A MAN?

MARSHAL   More than one!

KING   One will do!

MARSHAL   I mean, it's a...group of them...a kind of
BAND.

KING   Bring them all in.

(MARSHAL *hurries out, then music is heard which
gets louder as* MINSTREL BAND *comes in.*)

Let's just hope that *one* of them isn't married
already, that's all!

(MINSTREL BAND *marches round the arena, singing –
see p. 69 for music.*)

BAND   We're a merry band of minstrels marching free,
We're a merry band of minstrels full of glee,
We're a merry band of minstrels,
Merry band of minstrels,
A merry band of minstrels marching free.

(MINSTREL BAND *marches into formation before the
King.*)

Now a merry band of minstrels greets the King,
Now a merry band of minstrels dance and sing,
We're a merry band of minstrels,
Merry band of minstrels,
A merry band of minstrels greets the King.

KING   (*looking pleased*) Welcome, Minstrels! (*to Marshal*)
We'll sit over here. (*to Minstrel Band*) Go on! Go
on! We need cheering up.

(*Leader of Minstrel Band,* PRINCE ALEXANDER *in
disguise, bows and continues solo.*)

ALEXANDER   I'm the leader of the merry minstrel band,
I can entertain the people of the land,
I can entertain the people,
Entertain the people,
I'm the leader of the merry minstrel band.

I'm...(*He starts next verse but* KING *breaks in and
puts up his hand.*)

16

KING	Bravo! Bravo! You have a very fine band, my friend. And you have a very fine voice.
QUEEN	(*clapping*) Yes! Yes! Very fine...don't you think so, Leonora?
LEONORA	I suppose his voice is less boring than most of the voices in this Court.
KING	(*nodding in agreement*) That's high praise from my daughter, for she's not easy to please! You've sung so well that I have it in mind to give you a splendid reward. That is...(*whispering loudly to Alexander*)...as long as you're not married.
ALEXANDER	(*in surprise*) Married! No...I'm not married, your Majesty.
KING	Splendid! By the way...(*whispers*) what's your name?
ALEXANDER	(*pausing*) I'm Alex, the leader of the minstrels. Let me introduce...Hans.
HANS	(*bowing*) Honoured, your Majesty!
ALEXANDER	Herman...and Skuld.
HERMAN, SKULD	(*bowing*) Honoured, your Majesty!
KING	This is my wife, the Queen.
BAND	Your gracious Majesty.
KING	(*taking a deep breath*) And my daughter, Leonora.
BAND	(*admiringly*) Mmm! Mmm!
KING	Now about the reward...As I said, I have it in mind to give you a reward...A SIMPLY SPLENDID REWARD!
BAND	(*hopefully*) What is it?
KING	Well, it's for your leader, Alex, really. (*staring at Alex*) Alex, leader of the minstrels, I GIVE YOU...THE HAND OF MY DAUGHTER... IN MARRIAGE.

ALL	OH!
LEONORA	(*screaming*) Father! FATHER! (*pointing*) A common man from the streets – a wandering musician – without a title and WITH A BEARD!
QUEEN	(*sobbing*) Oh! No! No!
KING	(*taking Alexander's hand*) You can hardly refuse a King's gift.
ALEXANDER	(*stroking beard*) I don't want to, your Majesty. (*walking round Leonora*) I don't want to.
LEONORA	(*yells*) How dare you look at me like that?
ALEXANDER	(*to Band*) She's got a good, strong voice, don't you think?
HANS	Yes!
HERMAN	Just what we want!
SKULD	A girl to join the Band! A girl's voice for the Band!
KING	(*excitedly*) You'll take her then?
ALEXANDER	(*slapping palm of King's hand*) It's a deal!
	(MINSTRELS *drag* LEONORA *out.*)
LEONORA	(*screaming*) A deal! A deal! ME! A DEAL! Oh! Oh!
	(KING, *looking happy, and* QUEEN, *sobbing, go out.*)
MARSHAL	(*as he goes out*) A bad deal, if you ask me!
ARTIST	So the proud Leonora was married next day, And the Minstrel Band took her away, far away. (*pauses*) But...it was nothing but trouble, nothing but strife, Now that proud Leonora was Alex's wife.
	(HANS, HERMAN *and* SKULD *come in, holding up clothes.*)

18

HANS	Look at these trousers!
HERMAN	Look at my coat!
SKULD	And my shirt!
HANS	Leonora has sewn up the bottoms of these trouser legs.
HERMAN	And the pockets of this coat.
SKULD	And burnt an enormous hole in my best shirt.
HANS	(*putting arms down trouser legs*) Look at them! Oh well! I did tell her to sew up all the holes. But you know what she'll say if we complain.
HERMAN, SKULD	(*mimicking Leonora*) I wasn't brought up to be a servant!
HANS	Let's call her.
ALL	Leonora! LEONORA! (*All laugh as* LEONORA *appears.*)
LEONORA	Now what's the matter?
	(ALL *hold up clothes.*)
	I can't help it. I wasn't brought up to be a servant...
	(ALL *laugh.*)
HANS	...or a cook!
HERMAN	That pudding you cooked for dinner (*patting stomach*) is still rolling round and round inside here. (*He groans.*)
SKULD	(*opening mouth*) I soon won't have a tooth left in my head.
HANS	(*pretending to be serious*) Gentlemen! I think the time has come to make a proper complaint. Ready...?
ALL	We, the friends of your husband Alex, complain that you're useless. You can't cook...you can't...

19

(LEONORA *starts to cry.*)

LEONORA It's too bad. I do my best, but...I wasn't brought up to be a servant.

(*Enter* ALEXANDER.)

ALEXANDER What's the matter now? What have you three been doing to Leonora?

ALL (*winking at Alexander*) Us! DOING?

HANS No! It's the other way round. Leonora has been ill-treating US.

HERMAN (*holding stomach*) My poor stomach!

SKULD And my poor teeth.

ALL She's USELESS!

ALEXANDER What do you expect me to do about it?

ALL (*laughing*) SEND HER BACK!

ALEXANDER (*shaking head*) Can't be done, I'm afraid. The last words her father said to me were, 'Whatever happens, my dear fellow, she's yours for keeps, so don't bring her back.'

LEONORA (*sobbing noisily*) It's too bad! It's too bad!

ALL (*mimicking*) I wasn't brought up to be a servant!

ALEXANDER (*to Leonora*) The trouble with you, my dear, is that you weren't brought up to be anything useful.

HANS You can't sew!

HERMAN You can't cook!

SKULD And you can't sing!

ALL (*making faces at each other with fingers in ears*) She can't sing!

ALEXANDER (*sighing*) You're quite useless.

LEONORA (*crying angrily*) Useless! ME! USELESS!

20

ALEXANDER Mmm! Quite useless. So...I really don't think I can keep you any longer.

LEONORA (*beginning to look worried*) What do you mean?

ALEXANDER I mean what I said. I really don't think I can keep you any longer. I just wonder what is to become of you.

LEONORA You HAVE to look after me. You are my husband.

ALEXANDER Sorry! It can't be done. I'll just have to find somewhere to put you.

LEONORA PUT me! I'm staying with you.

ALEXANDER Well, I'm not STAYING! I'm going! (*winking at others*) And the Minstrels are going with me.

LEONORA If you're going, I'm going.

ALEXANDER Very well! I'll give you one last chance to make yourself useful. You've got a pretty face, so you can go round with the box and collect the money.

HANS Where are we going today, Alex?

ALEXANDER We're off to play at Prince Alexander's Castle.

ALL (*excitedly*) Three cheers! The Castle!

LEONORA (*horrified*) Not at PRINCE ALEXANDER'S Castle!

ALL Why not?

LEONORA Because I might be recognised. Once...I met...I mean...There will be lots of people at Prince Alexander's Castle.

HANS Ooooh! Leonora! Did you ever meet Prince Alexander?

HERMAN (*winking at Alexander*) I wonder...was Prince Alexander ever one of your suitors?

(ALEXANDER *walks to one side and laughs with* HERMAN.)

SKULD	Hey! I've had an idea! Perhaps Prince Alexander would give Leonora a job at his Castle!
LEONORA	(*terrified*) No! No! I can't go to the Castle.
ALEXANDER	Leonora! A few minutes ago you said, 'If you're going, I'm going.' So now you're going to the Castle. Come on!

(MINSTRELS *drag* LEONORA *off.*)

ARTIST	The guests at the Castle began to appear, As the Prince, with his friends and the lady, drew near. But...plead as she did. cry as she did, the Prince wouldn't heed her.

(PAGE *and other* CASTLE SERVANTS *come in, carrying a table on which they put glasses, bottles of wine and other drinks.*)

PAGE	What a feast we'll have! (*looking at bottles*) Ah! I'll try a little of this. (*He drinks.*) Mmm! Beautiful!

(LORD CHAMBERLAIN *hurries in.*)

CHAMBERLAIN	Page! Page! The guests are on their way, but the Band hasn't arrived.
PAGE	Don't worry, Lord Chamberlain. (*taking another sip*) I never do! I'll bring the guests in here for a drink. (*He goes out.*)
CHAMBERLAIN	I'll go this way and see if the Band has arrived. (*He hurries out.*)

(PAGE *brings in a large party of guests, including the* DUKES, LORDS *and* EARL.)

PAGE	(*waving towards table*) Your Excellencies! My Lords! Ladies and Gentlemen! On behalf of His Royal Highness, the Prince Alexander, I bid you all welcome!
HANOVER, GRENA	(*hurrying towards table*) Ah! Refreshments! (*They help themselves.*)

HAMBURG	This is better, Frankie. Not like the last place we were in.
FRANKFURT	No horrible princesses! I hope! Do you remember how rude Leonora was to us?
ROOS	Mmm! I wonder who the King managed to marry her off to?
ALL OLD SUITORS	(*raising glasses*) Good luck to him, whoever it is!
ROOS	(*looking round*) Do you know, I wouldn't mind staying here for a bit. FREE, of course!
ALL OLD SUITORS	(*raising glasses*) FREE!
	(CHAMBERLAIN *comes in, holding* LEONORA *by the arm.*)
CHAMBERLAIN	(*hisses to Page*) They've come. They're just getting their instruments ready. (*to Leonora*) Come along, my dear. Your Band is to play to our guests in this room.
LEONORA	(*looking round and then putting hands over face in horror*) Oh! They're all here! (*She runs to side of arena and counts on fingers.*) Dumpling…Bean Pole…Tub…Whitewash…Rooster…that's five and there were six. (*looking round fearfully*) No… Prince Alexander…No PRICKLY BEARD.
CHAMBERLAIN	(*to Leonora*) Whatever's the matter?
LEONORA	I don't know what to do. (*pulling scarf half over face*) What shall I do?
CHAMBERLAIN	(*going over to her*) Why are you covering your face with that scarf? You've got a very pretty face, so let people see it.
LEONORA	No! No! I've got chicken-pox!
CHAMBERLAIN	(*surprised*) You hadn't got it a few minutes ago!
LEONORA	Chicken-pox always comes on very quickly with me.

23

CHAMBERLAIN	What do you mean, girl? You can't have chicken-pox more than once.
LEONORA	I do! I'm always having it. Besides...it's catching. I...I...I'd better stay away from everyone – OVER HERE. (*She moves to side holding scarf over face.*)
PAGE	(*holding up both hands*) Your Excellencies! My Lords! Ladies and Gentlemen! (*looking off stage*) Pray silence for His Royal Highness, the Prince Alexander.
	(ALL *make deep bows as* PRINCE ALEXANDER *comes in, followed by* HANS, HERMAN *and* SKULD *in Court dress.*)
ALL	(*raising glasses*) The Prince Alexander!
ALEXANDER	(*taking glass and raising it*) I bid you all welcome. Your good health!
CHAMBERLAIN	(*rushing over to Alexander*) Your Highness! It's not good health. We've got a case of chicken-pox in here and it's terribly catching.
ALL	(*looking at each other*) CHICKEN-POX!
ALEXANDER	One of my guests with chicken-pox! Good gracious! I'm surprised he accepted the invitation.
	(*All look suspiciously at each other.*)
CHAMBERLAIN	Not one of your guests, Prince. One of the Minstrel Band.
ALEXANDER	Oh really! (*looking round*) I don't see the Band anywhere.
CHAMBERLAIN	(*pointing accusing finger*) Over THERE!
	(*Everyone moves away from Leonora as she cowers with scarf over face.*)
ALEXANDER	Oh! The young lady! (*to page*) Bring her over to me, page.

PAGE   But Highness, she says she's got chicken-pox.

ALEXANDER   Oh, does she! (*moving towards Leonora*) I'll see for myself.

(LEONORA *begins to cry as* ALEXANDER *pulls away scarf.*)

LEONORA   Please! Please! I didn't mean it. (*wailing*) I didn't mean to call you Prickly Beard, Prince Alexander.

ALEXANDER   Perhaps, my dear Leonora, you should call me... Alex, from now on.

LEONORA   (*touching Alexander's beard*) Alex...Alex! Oh! It is the same beard.

ALEXANDER   Yes, and it is the same man!

LEONORA   Prince Alexander...Alex, leader of the Minstrel Band. I don't quite understand.

ALEXANDER   I think you do, my dear. I had to cure you of your pride.

LEONORA   Oh, Alexander...(*taking his hand*)

ALEXANDER   (*to all*) So...now give welcome to our PRINCESS LEONORA!

ALL   (*raising glasses*) THE PRINCESS LEONORA!

(PRINCE ALEXANDER *leads* PRINCESS LEONORA *out, followed by* SUITORS, GUESTS *and others.*)

ARTIST   So proud Leonora, a meek loving wife,
Was humble and good...for the rest of her life.

END OF FIRST PLAY

PLAYWATCHERS

People of Cassel

JACOB *and* WILHELM GRIMM *leave the others and walk over to the bench.*

JACOB We have a new tale now, brother.

WILHELM And it's all written down. (*He points to his notebook.*)

JACOB I think you are right about the book, Wilhelm. Story-tellers such as this artist fellow, are getting fewer.

WILHELM So we must travel to each town and catch these stories while they are still alive!

JACOB (*laughing*) You make it sound as if we are to catch butterflies!

(OLD SOLDIER *comes in.*)

But look who's coming towards us. It's that old soldier we listened to in Marburg some weeks ago.

WILHELM (*waving hand*) So you've travelled the road from Marburg, old friend?

OLD SOLDIER You remember me, then?

JACOB Certainly! You told us the tale of the Valiant Little Tailor.

WILHELM (*showing notebook*) Look! I wrote it all down.

OLD SOLDIER   (*reading*) The Valiant Little Tailor! So...(*grinning*) the Old Soldier will leave something to the world when all is done. But it's a poor living! (*He points to his ragged trousers, then goes on hopefully.*) Many's the tale I've told for a new pair of trousers.

JACOB   (*slapping Old Soldier on the back*) Then let's trade a new pair of trousers for yet another story, Soldier.

WILHELM   (*beckoning onlookers*) Over here! Come and listen! The Old Soldier of Marburg has a tale to tell.

OLD SOLDIER   (*settling himself on bench*) Well now! (*to listeners*) Is it a tale you're waiting for?

LISTENERS   We are! We are!

OLD SOLDIER   Once there was a king called Osmund, who wasn't the usual sort of king at all. He thought of nothing but his horses...He dreamed of them by night, he rode them by day, and quite forgot that there were bills to pay.

Here begins The story of Straw into Gold.

The Story of Straw into Gold

Playmakers

KING OSMUND

CHIEF OF HORSE
NIMMO – a stable boy

CAPTAIN of the King's Guard
Other Guards

FIRST CORN MERCHANT
SECOND CORN MERCHANT
THIRD CORN MERCHANT

MILLER
EVA – his daughter
PIMM – his son

RUMPLESTILTSKIN – Master of the Kelpies, impish spirits
QUIN
ZAMBO
SQUIDGE Other Kelpies
VETCH
TWIZZLE

NURSE-MAID

The Story of Straw into Gold

The King's GUARDS *march into the arena.*

CAPTAIN One! Two! One! Two!

ALL GUARDS (*taking up marching rhythm*) One! Two! One! Two! (*marching continues*)

CAPTAIN TURN! (*marching continues to Guards' count*) HALT! Stand at ... EASE!

(*Voices are heard as drill ends and* GUARDS *move to side of arena.*)

WHO GOES THERE?

MERCHANTS FRIENDS!

CAPTAIN GIVE THE PASSWORD!

(*Enter* CORN MERCHANTS.)

FIRST MERCHANT You know us!

SECOND MERCHANT We come here often enough!

THIRD MERCHANT And go away again – without our money!

FIRST MERCHANT But not this time, captain. (*waving bill*) We're staying here until we're paid.

CAPTAIN It's nothing to do with me. The King pays the bills.

ALL MERCHANTS Oh no, he doesn't!

FIRST MERCHANT That's the trouble! So ...(*pointing to ground*) we're staying right here.

CAPTAIN You can't stay here!

ALL MERCHANTS Who says so?

CAPTAIN I say so! You're tradesmen!

ALL MERCHANTS Right! (*They whisper to each other and then sit down.*)

29

CAPTAIN	You can't do that.
ALL MERCHANTS	We've done it!
CAPTAIN	I'm warning you! I shall put it in my report and that goes...TO THE KING.
FIRST MERCHANT	Good! The sooner we see the King, the better!
CAPTAIN	The King is...out riding.
FIRST MERCHANT	Yes! The King is out riding on a horse, which is full of OUR corn.
ALL MERCHANTS	And not paid for!

(*Sounds of horses' hooves are heard.* GUARDS *jump to attention and* MERCHANTS *get up, rubbing hands together.*)

NOW THEN!

(KING OSMUND *comes in with his* CHIEF OF HORSE *and* NIMMO.)

KING OSMUND	The grey horses need more corn, Chief of Horse. You'd better double their rations.
CHIEF OF HORSE	We're very short of corn, Sire.
KING OSMUND	Nimmo! Give my chestnut another bucket of oats.
NIMMO	(*opening hands*) But...
KING OSMUND	Go on, Nimmo. Do it!

(NIMMO *shrugs and goes out.*)

CAPTAIN	(*pointing to merchants*) Sire! These men have been making a nuisance of themselves.
KING OSMUND	(*looking at merchants*) Oh! What do you want?
ALL MERCHANTS	(*holding up bills*) Our money!
FIRST MERCHANT	You owe me for...one hundred sacks of corn, King.
SECOND MERCHANT	And you owe me for...two hundred sacks of maize.

30

THIRD MERCHANT	And me for...three hundred and fifty sacks of oats.
KING OSMUND	All right! All right!
FIRST MERCHANT	But it's not all right!
ALL MERCHANTS	It's all wrong!
KING OSMUND	You can...um...come back tomorrow. (*He signs to captain.*)
ALL MERCHANTS	(*angrily*) It's always tomorrow!
CAPTAIN	GUARDS!
	(GUARDS *move forward.*)
KING OSMUND	Come back tomorrow at the same time and...I'll see what I can do.
	(GUARDS *push* MERCHANTS *back towards gate.*)
ALL MERCHANTS	Tomorrow! (*grumbling to each other*) It's always tomorrow! (*They go out.*)
KING OSMUND	(*taking out empty money bag*) Empty! And it will be just as empty tomorrow. (*to Chief of Horse*) You'll have to find some new corn merchants without delay.
CHIEF OF HORSE	Impossible, Sire! We owe money to every merchant in the country.
KING OSMUND	(*sighing*) If only there were some way out... (*thoughtfully*) There must be some way out.
CHIEF OF HORSE	Well Sire, you could look for a rich wife!
KING OSMUND	(*groaning*) I'd rather look for a new horse than a wife any day. (*sighing*) Do you realise, Chief of Horse, that I would need to change all the straw in my stables into gold, to pay off my debts?
	(NIMMO *rushes in.*)
NIMMO	Your Majesty! We're saved! I mean the horses are saved. (*pointing to gate*) There's a miller outside – a MILLER!

KING OSMUND	Aha! Millers have plenty of corn...
CHIEF OF HORSE	Mmm! (*to Nimmo*) But does he know...? (*He shows his empty pockets.*)
NIMMO	He wants to put the King's coat of arms on his mill. So!!
KING OSMUND	(*rubbing hands together*) Marvellous! Fetch him in, Nimmo.

(NIMMO *rushes out.*)

Now I won't have to bother to look for a rich wife – not at the moment, anyway!

(MILLER *comes in, followed by his son* PIMM *and* NIMMO.)

MILLER	I hear you want my corn, your Majesty. Have as much as you like, your Majesty. I shall be honoured...
CHIEF OF HORSE	(*whispers to Nimmo*) But not paid!
KING OSMUND	Thank you, my man. See to it, Chief of Horse. (*He begins to go out.*)
MILLER	Majesty! Majesty! First, may I make a request?
KING OSMUND	Request? Ah yes! A coat of arms! Have as many coats of arms as you like, Miller.
MILLER	Majesty! Allow me to introduce my son, Pimm.
KING OSMUND	Pimm, Ah yes! Good day to you, Pimm. (*He begins to walk out again.*)
PIMM	(*bowing*) Good day to your Majesty.
MILLER	(*running after King*) Your Majesty!

(KING *stops and turns as* MILLER *hisses to* PIMM.)

Fetch your sister!

(PIMM *runs out.*)

Allow me to introduce my daughter, Eva, to your Majesty.

KING OSMUND	(*looking round*) Where is she? I can't see her.
MILLER	She's on her way, your Majesty.
CHIEF OF HORSE	Look here, Miller, the King can't spend all day waiting to meet your family.
MILLER	This is the last one, I promise. But my Eva has always wanted to meet your Majesty and... (*cunningly*) I am supplying the corn.
CHIEF OF HORSE	Ah yes! Of course! Is this Eva of yours a pretty girl, Miller?
MILLER	She's more beautiful than words can describe, my Lord. And clever! Why, there's nothing my Eva can't do.
CHIEF OF HORSE	(*to King*) I think we can say that this Miller is proud of his daughter, Sire!
MILLER	Oh, I am! My Eva can cook and sew...and spin...She can spin a thread so finely that it is...pure gold.
CHIEF OF HORSE	That must be useful! I suppose you'll be telling us next that this daughter of yours can spin straw into gold! (*turning to King and laughing*) That could be VERY useful!
MILLER	Oh, yes! She can do that!
ALL	WHAT?
	(PIMM *comes in with his sister* EVA.)
MILLER	(*proudly*) Majesty! Allow me to introduce my daughter, Eva.
EVA	(*curtseying*) I'm honoured, your Majesty.
KING OSMUND	Good day to you, Eva. Come on now, Chief of Horse, we'll go back to the horses. (*He begins to go out again.*)
CHIEF OF HORSE	(*giving Eva a quick look*) You were quite right, Miller. She's a very pretty girl. Now off we go. (*He follows King.*)

MILLER	(*shouting after them*) She can do ANYTHING, your honour!
CHIEF OF HORSE	(*calling back*) So you said!
MILLER	(*shouting after them*) Anything! She can...SPIN STRAW INTO GOLD!

(KING *and* CHIEF OF HORSE *come back.*)

CHIEF OF HORSE	(*to King*) He's serious, you know.
KING OSMUND	All right, Miller. As that is your boast, we'll put your daughter to the test.
EVA	No! NO!
MILLER	(*to Eva*) Be quiet, girl! You never know...The King might...
PIMM	(*looking worried*) Father! No!
MILLER	(*to Pimm*) Be quiet, you young fool! (*to Eva*) The King might take a fancy to you. Just think, Eva...(*whispering*) he might MARRY you.
EVA	But you know I can't...
CHIEF OF HORSE	Guards! Put this girl in the stable with the straw and lock the door.
KING	(*laughing*) And make sure you've spun all the straw in the stable into gold by the time I come back from my ride, or...or it will be the worse for you!

(GUARDS *push* EVA *into stable, then go out.*)

Now...at last...to the horses! (*He strides out.*)

CHIEF OF HORSE	(*jabbing finger at Miller*) And see that the corn is delivered or...it will be the worse for you! (*He follows King out.*)
PIMM	(*in worried voice*) Father! How could you do that to Eva?

NIMMO	(*jabbing finger at Pimm*) Get that corn or...it will be the worse for all of you! (*He follows Chief of Horse out.*)
	(EVA's *sobs are heard from stable.*)
PIMM	Listen! What will happen to her?
MILLER	With a bit of luck, the King will take a fancy to Eva and want to marry her. (*excitedly*) Just imagine! My Eva married to the King. (*He rushes out.*)
PIMM	Eva is so sweet and good. (*More sobs are heard from stable.*) My poor sister! What will she do?
	(RUMPLESTILTSKIN *hobbles in and hides behind a corn bin.*)
	No-one can spin straw into gold. I can't leave her. (*He looks round.*) I'll stay for a while. (*He sits behind another corn bin as Eva's sobs become louder.*)
RUMPLESTILTSKIN	(*hobbling forward*) Who's there? (*rapping on stable door with stick*) Anybody at home?
EVA	(*between sobs*) Who...is...it?
RUMPLESTILTSKIN	Open the door and you will see.
EVA	I can't. I'm locked in.
RUMPLESTILTSKIN	(*cackling*) Aha! Maybe this is my chance! (*putting key in lock*) Magic key! Open for me! (*He opens the door.*)
EVA	(*running out*) I'm free! (*seeing Rumplestiltskin*) AaaahhhH! Who are you? Are you friendly?
RUMPLESTILTSKIN	(*cunningly*) Maybe I am...maybe I'm not. Tell me, girl, why are you crying?
EVA	The King has set me an impossible task. He says I must spin all the straw in that stable (*pointing*) into GOLD!

RUMPLESTILTSKIN	(*cackling*) Aha! This IS my chance. Tell me, girl, what will you give me if I do it for you?
EVA	Anything! But...you can't do it, can you?
RUMPLESTILTSKIN	Will you give me your necklace?
EVA	Willingly! I'll give you anything in the world, little old man.
RUMPLESTILTSKIN	(*hobbling into stable and shutting door*) Then I'll do it for your necklace.
EVA	I can't believe that he can do it. Listen! What a strange little song he's singing.
RUMPLESTILTSKIN	(*chanting from stable*) Fi-fo-fum, And three-two-one, Hi-ho-hum, And spin-span-spun. Hee-hi-hold, That's how it's done, STRAW INTO GOLD! And fortune won.
EVA	Straw into gold! I can't believe it!
	(RUMPLESTILTSKIN *hobbles out of stable, carrying a large reel of gold thread.*)
RUMPLESTILTSKIN	There! Pure gold thread.
EVA	That's wonderful. (*eagerly*) Tell me your secret. Tell me how you did it, little old man.
RUMPLESTILTSKIN	No! It is a secret that can never be told.
EVA	(*looking round nervously*) There's someone coming. Here! (*giving necklace to Rumplestiltskin*) Take this! But go! Quickly! (*She hurries back into stable.*)
	(RUMPLESTILTSKIN *hobbles back to hiding place.* KING, CHIEF OF HORSE *and* NIMMO *come in and look over stable door.*)

36

KING OSMUND	Good gracious! Look! I do believe she's done it!
CHIEF OF HORSE	(*to Nimmo*) Let her out, Nimmo.

(NIMMO *takes key and unlocks door.* EVA *comes out carrying reel of gold thread.*)

	You're right, Sire. And to think we didn't believe that boastful Miller.
NIMMO	(*running fingers through thread*) It's pure gold thread, your Majesty.
EVA	(*to King*) Now please, your Majesty, let me go home.
KING OSMUND	Go home! Let a clever girl like you go home! Not likely! If you can do it once, you can do it again!
EVA	(*beginning to cry*) You don't understand...I can't...
CHIEF OF HORSE	She's a very pretty girl, Sire, when she's not crying.
KING OSMUND	(*putting finger under Eva's chin*) So she is! Now, my dear, dry your tears and listen to this! If you can spin another stable full of straw into gold... YOU SHALL MARRY ME AND BE MY QUEEN!
EVA	Queen! QUEEN! (*half to herself*) I can't believe it! I can't believe it! But my father did say...
CHIEF OF HORSE	(*nodding*) So that was the Miller's little game!
KING OSMUND	(*to Chief of Horse*) Just think! I shall be able to pay off all my debts.
EVA	(*nervously*) But perhaps I shan't be able to do it...this time.

(CHIEF OF HORSE *and* NIMMO *push* EVA *into a second stable and lock the door.*)

KING OSMUND	(*laughing*) Then it will be OFF with your head!

(*They go out laughing and* PIMM *creeps from his hiding place and looks round.*)

PIMM I don't like this! I don't like it at all. (*calls*) Eva! Eva! Are you all right?

EVA (*from stable*) Who's that?

PIMM It's me! Pimm! (*looking round*) Oh! That little old man's coming back!

(*Pimm returns to hiding place as* RUMPLESTILTSKIN *hobbles towards second stable door.*)

EVA (*from stable*) Who is it? Please…is it you, little old man?

RUMPLESTILTSKIN (*cackling*) Maybe it is…maybe it isn't. Ha-ha-ha!

EVA (*from stable*) Open the door, please!

RUMPLESTILTSKIN (*putting key in lock*)
Magic key!
Open for me! (*He opens the door.*)

EVA (*coming out*) Thank goodness you've come back. Look! (*points to stable*) More straw for you to spin into gold. (*She pushes Rumplestiltskin.*) Go on! Hurry up!

RUMPLESTILTSKIN Not so fast, my girl. (*looking into stable*) But there's much more this time.

EVA Please…because…(*excitedly*) the King is going to MARRY me. At least, he will when all this straw is spun into gold.

RUMPLESTILTSKIN (*cunningly*) What will you give me if I do it?

EVA Oh, I don't know. You see…(*showing she has no jewels*) I'm only a poor Miller's daughter…

RUMPLESTILTSKIN (*cackling*)…who wants to be Queen! Aha! Now IS my chance! (*to Eva*) NO PAY…NO WORK!

EVA Listen! When I'm Queen I shall be very rich…so you can let me pay later.

RUMPLESTILTSKIN	Later...Ah! I wonder what you can give me... later?
EVA	I'll give you anything you ask for...anything in the world. I promise!
RUMPLESTILTSKIN	(*holding up palm of hand*) Put your hand on mine. (EVA *does so.*) Say: I PROMISE TO GIVE YOU...
EVA	(*repeats*) I promise to give you...
RUMPLESTILTSKIN	...ANYTHING YOU ASK FOR...
EVA	(*repeats*)...anything you ask for...
RUMPLESTILTSKIN	(*softly*)...MY FIRST...
EVA	(*repeats*)...My first...
RUMPLESTILTSKIN	CHILD!
EVA	Child! CHILD! (*in horror*) MY FIRST CHILD!
RUMPLESTILTSKIN	(*hobbling into stable and cackling to himself*) Your first child!
EVA	My first child! Oh dear! What have I promised?
RUMPLESTILTSKIN	(*chanting from stable*) Fi-fo-fum, And three-two-one, Hi-ho-hum, And spin-span-spun. Hee-hi-hold, That's how it's done, STRAW INTO GOLD! And fortune won.
EVA	STRAW INTO GOLD! I do believe he's done it again! Oh well! I may never have a child!
RUMPLESTILTSKIN	(*hobbling out carrying a large reel of gold thread*) There! (*putting reel on ground*) Pure gold thread! The rest of it...(*pointing*) is inside.
EVA	This time you must tell me your secret, little old man.

RUMPLESTILTSKIN	No! It is a secret that can never be told.
EVA	(*crossly*) You won't tell me anything. Why! I don't even know your name. What is your name?
RUMPLESTILTSKIN	My name is a secret that can never be told.
EVA	(*stamping foot*) Don't tell me then! I don't care! (*holding head up high*) Anyway! I'm going to be Queen.
RUMPLESTILTSKIN	(*hobbling away*) DON'T CARE was MADE TO CARE, so...Miller's daughter...BEWARE!
EVA	Me! Queen! Me! (*looking round*) Ah! They're coming back.

(EVA *goes back into stable as* KING OSMUND, CHIEF OF HORSE *and* NIMMO *hurry in and look over stable door.*)

NIMMO	Look! She's done it again.
CHIEF OF HORSE	Let her out, Nimmo.

(NIMMO *takes key and* EVA *comes out carrying reel.*)

So...(*to King*) what about your promise, Sire?

KING OSMUND	(*putting finger under Eva's chin*) Well, she's a very pretty girl...and clever! I shall be pleased to marry her. Now come along everybody, back to the horses!
EVA	But what about the wedding?
KING OSMUND	Don't worry, my dear. We'll have a wonderful wedding. All this gold...and a pretty girl. It's my lucky day! (*taking Eva's hand*) Come along, my dear.

(*They all go out and* PIMM *creeps from his hiding place.*)

PIMM	Just like my father said! All the same, I don't feel happy about it. That little old man said 'Miller's

daughter, BEWARE!' I'm going after him. I'm going to find out more about him. (*He hurries out.*)

OLD SOLDIER So Eva married the King...(*pause*) But Pimm, her brother, roamed far and wide looking for that little old man. And then...at last...one night, deep in a forest, he happened to hear voices.

(PIMM *comes in and stays hidden at side.* RUMPLESTILTSKIN *dances to centre of arena, using his stick as third leg, followed by his* KELPIES.)

KELPIES Round and round we Kelpies go,
Randon-random, hee-hi-ho!
Merrily we dance around
In this place, our secret ground.
Randon-random, hee-hi-ho!
Round and round we Kelpies go.

RUMPLESTILTSKIN (*lying down*) Kelpies!

KELPIES Yes, Master?

RUMPLESTILTSKIN My head itches! Scratch my head, Quin.

QUIN Quin will do it, Master. Quin is a good scratcher.

RUMPLESTILTSKIN You scratch my right foot, Zambo. And you scratch the other one, Squidge.

ZAMBO, SQUIDGE Yes, Master!

RUMPLESTILTSKIN Now my hands itch.

(VETCH *and* TWIZZLE *rush to scratch a hand each.*)

VETCH That means money, Master!

TWIZZLE (*jumping and twirling round*) Money! Money! Money!

RUMPLESTILTSKIN (*sitting up and scattering Kelpies*) No! Not money!

KELPIES What then, Master?

RUMPLESTILTSKIN (*scratching nose*) My nose tells me...and my nose is never wrong...that THE TIME HAS COME!

KELPIES What time, Master?

41

RUMPLESTILTSKIN	The time has come, Kelpies, for a GREAT CELEBRATION.
KELPIES	What for, Master?
RUMPLESTILTSKIN	(*cackling*) Guess!
KELPIES	You've learnt a new spell! (*They try other guesses.*)
RUMPLESTILTSKIN	(*cackling*) No! Your old Master is getting himself a...(*He rocks arms to and fro.*)
KELPIES	(*rocking arms and looking at each other*) Our old Master is getting us a...
RUMPLESTILTSKIN	(*cackling*) Merrily we'll dance and sing, Tomorrow will a stranger bring! (*He does his three-legged dance and all sing.*)
KELPIES	Merrily the feast we'll make, Tomorrow brew, tomorrow bake, Merrily we'll dance and sing, For next day will a stranger bring.
RUMPLESTILTSKIN	(*hobbling forward*) The next day will a stranger bring...You'll see...(*He waves his stick as* KELPIES *go out.*) My nose tells me that my lady's time has come. There will be a baby now – as sure as my name is RUMPLESTILTSKIN! (*cackles*) At last! My chance to have a HUMAN...(*He rocks his arms as he hobbles out.*)
	(PIMM *goes out the other way.*)
OLD SOLDIER	At the Palace a whole year passed and a child was born to Eva. But every time she looked at her baby son, she was troubled. For she remembered the promise she had made to the little old man.
	(EVA *comes in and sits in centre of arena while* NURSE-MAID *rocks baby in arms.*)
NURSE-MAID	Oh, what a beautiful baby!
EVA	(*sadly*) Mmmm.

42

NURSE-MAID	Your Majesty! (*touches Eva's sleeve*) Wouldn't you like to hold him?
EVA	(*shivering*) Give the baby to me, then. (*shivering*) Oh dear! I am so cold.
NURSE-MAID	I'll run and get you a fur wrap. (*She gives the baby to Eva, then runs out.*)
EVA	(*looking at baby and sighing*) I have the most beautiful baby in the world but I feel so cold and sad...and...
	(EVA *begins to cry as* RUMPLESTILTSKIN *hobbles in.*)
RUMPLESTILTSKIN	(*cackling*) What! Still crying, my lady?
EVA	(*jumping up in horror*) YOU!
RUMPLESTILTSKIN	Why are you crying? (*cackling*) Don't you like your baby? (*He bends over the baby.*)
EVA	(*drawing away*) Keep away from my baby. Keep away!
RUMPLESTILTSKIN	Remember your promise, Miller's daughter. (*holding out arms*) Give the child to me.
EVA	(*holding the baby close*) Never! Never! Never! You can have all the riches in the kingdom, but...
RUMPLESTILTSKIN	(*stamping foot angrily*) I don't want your riches. I can spin straw into gold...remember? I want something LIVING. Give him to me!
EVA	(*holding baby tightly*) There must be something else. There must be!
RUMPLESTILTSKIN	(*scratching head*) Maybe there is...(*cackling*) maybe there isn't.
EVA	Please! PLEASE!
RUMPLESTILTSKIN	(*cunningly*) I'll tell you what I'll do. I'll sit over there under that bush and watch the child, and IF YOU CAN GUESS MY NAME BEFORE NIGHTFALL, I'll let you off your promise!

	(*hobbles to side*) But she'll never guess my name. Never! Never! Never! (*He cackles to himself.*)
EVA	Guess his name before nightfall! That's impossible. Oh, what shall I do? There are so many names.

(NURSE-MAID *comes in, carrying wrap.*)

NURSE-MAID	Now you will feel better, your Majesty.
EVA	Not until I have his name.
NURSE-MAID	(*looking at baby*) But the baby has a name already...Osmund, after his father.
EVA	I mean...I mean...(*quickly*) I want to give him a *second* name. Go to the King's library and fetch the book called, 'All the Christian names in the world'.

(NURSE-MAID *hurries out.*)

There are hundreds of names in that.

(RUMPLESTILTSKIN *hobbles out from bush.*)

RUMPLESTILTSKIN	What's my name, Miller's daughter. (*cackling*) Why don't you go through the alphabet?
EVA	Yes, yes! Now, let me see...A is for Adam...and Adolphus...and Archibald...Is your name Archibald?
RUMPLESTILTSKIN	(*hugging himself with glee*) No, that's not my name! Why don't you try...Z!

(As NURSE-MAID *comes in carrying large, labelled book,* RUMPLESTILTSKIN *hurries back to bush.*)

EVA	(*to Nurse-Maid*) Quick! Find letter Z at the back of the book.
NURSE-MAID	(*turning pages*) There aren't many Zs, my lady. ZACH-A-RIAH! (*laughing*) That's a strange name!

EVA	A STRANGE name! Yes! (*excitedly*) Go and fetch 'All the strange names in the world', from the King's library.
	(NURSE-MAID *hurries out.*)
	That's...(*hopefully*) where his name could be.
	(RUMPLESTILTSKIN *hobbles out.*)
RUMPLESTILTSKIN	Have you guessed my name yet, Miller's daughter?
EVA	Is your name...Zachariah?
RUMPLESTILTSKIN	No! (*rubbing hands*) That's not my name. (*cackling*) You'll never guess it! (*He goes back to bush.*)
	(NURSE-MAID *comes in carrying another large, labelled book.*)
NURSE-MAID	This is the one, your Majesty. And my lady, I have some news for you. Your brother, Pimm, has just arrived at the Palace gate.
EVA	Pimm? Oh! Go and fetch him. He'll help me to look for a name.
	(NURSE-MAID *goes out as* EVA *frantically turns pages of book.*)
	I'll try these beginning with B...this one...and this one...
	(RUMPLESTILTSKIN *hobbles out.*)
RUMPLESTILTSKIN	I'm still here, Miller's daughter.
EVA	I know! Your name is...Bullybags!
RUMPLESTILTSKIN	That's not my name! (*He cackles.*)
EVA	Bandylegs!
RUMPLESTILTSKIN	That's not my name! (*He cackles and rubs his hands.*)
EVA	Vinegar Tom!

RUMPLESTILTSKIN	That's not my name! (*He rubs his hands and dances in glee.*)
EVA	(*jumping up*) I know! It's Skillywidden!
RUMPLESTILTSKIN	No! You'll never get it. So I'll take the child now.
EVA	(*holding baby tightly cries*) Don't touch my child!
	(*As* RUMPLESTILTSKIN *tries to take the baby from Eva,* PIMM *comes in.*)
PIMM	What's going on?
RUMPLESTILTSKIN	(*shouts*) He's mine! The child is mine! Give him to me!
PIMM	(*rushing forward and seizing Rumplestiltskin*) Stop that! (*looking closely*) I've seen you before! I remember! You're that little old man who spun straw into gold...AND I SAW YOU IN THE FOREST!
RUMPLESTILTSKIN	(*angrily*) Get away! (*hitting out*) Get away!
PIMM	I remember! You're one of those Kelpies. You're their old Master...You're RUMPLESTILTSKIN!
EVA	Rumplestiltskin! So that's your name! RUMPLESTILTSKIN!
RUMPLESTILTSKIN	(*in a mad frenzy*) The Devil it is! The Devil it is! (*He stamps his foot very hard.*) OwwWWcchhHH! (*He hobbles out shouting and shaking fist at Eva and Pimm.*)
EVA, PIMM	(*calling after him*) And never come back! (*going out the other way*) NEVER COME BACK!

END OF SECOND PLAY

 # PLAYWATCHERS

People of Cassel

The LISTENERS *wander away from the bench, leaving* JACOB *and* WILHELM GRIMM *with the* OLD SOLDIER.

JACOB   That was a fine, strong story, Soldier!

WILHELM   But not a pretty tale!

OLD SOLDIER   Life is not always pretty, gentlemen. And old trousers are not pretty! (*showing holes*) Besides, they let in the wind.

JACOB   You shall have new trousers, Soldier, and a coat to keep out the wind.

(*Enter* EGG-WIFE.)

WILHELM   (*pointing*) Look who has come now, brother.

JACOB   (*getting up*) Ah! The good Egg-Wife of Cassel!

WILHELM   Our Fairy Tale Woman!

JACOB   (*to Old Soldier*) Here is a story-teller, Soldier, who can draw old men from the chimney corner...

WILHELM   ...and children from their play. (*They walk over to join others around the Egg-Wife.*) Good day to you, Frau! Have you got a story for us today?

EGG-WIFE   Wait and see, Wilhelm Grimm! I shall keep my tale safe inside my head for a while yet.

OLD SOLDIER   (*laughing*) Ho, ho! Is it safe in there, woman?

EGG-WIFE	Safer than in some heads, I reckon! (*looking round*) There are some who cannot keep anything in their heads from one day to the next!
JACOB	Good Frau! Don't tease us. Let's hear your tale.
EGG-WIFE	(*settling herself*) Are you all ready, then?
LISTENERS	We are! We are!
EGG-WIFE	This is the tale I have to tell, and this is the way I tell it. JUST SUPPOSE that...over OUR hill (*She points and all look.*) where the trees meet the sky, Old Mother Cat-Owl, wizened and grey, stalks the woods, searching for prey. JUST SUPPOSE that...down in *our* dell (*She points and all look.*) our children are playing...

Here begins The story of the Castle of Birds.

The Story of the Castle of Birds

Playmakers

ELSA ⎤
ELSINORE ⎥
AVA ⎥ Children of Castle Dell
HILD ⎥
GART ⎥
MENNI ⎦

CAT-OWL – a wicked witch

RAGGY-LIDDY – her servant

MAG – a magpie ⎤ other servants of Cat-Owl
BEL – a hare ⎦

JORINDA ⎤ a boy and girl who are strangers to Castle Dell
JORINDEL ⎦

FAIRY QUEEN

PEARL – a fairy

YELLOW FLOWER FAIRIES

BLUE FLOWER FAIRIES

RED FLOWER FAIRIES

Other fairies

The Story of the Castle of Birds

THE CHILDREN OF CASTLE DELL, *clapping their hands, follow* ELSA
into the arena.

ELSA (*zig-zagging*)
Follow me down the winding river,
Follow me down – with a shake and a shiver.

CHILDREN Follow her down – with a shake and a shiver!

ELSA (*climbing*)
Follow me up the grassy hill,
Follow me up – and then stand still.

CHILDREN Follow her up – and then stand still!

ELSA (*ducking*)
Follow me under the old oak gate,
Follow me under – what's your fate?

CHILDREN Follow her under – what's our fate?

ELSA (*jumping*)
Follow me over the waterfall,
Follow me NOW – or not at all?

CHILDREN Follow her NOW – or not at all?

ELSA (*looking round*)
Follow me onto... THE CASTLE STONES! (*She
jumps onto the first of some stepping stones leading
out of arena.*)

CHILDREN (*in horror*) No! No! No!

ELSINORE No, Elsa! You know that we must never go near
Cat-Owl's castle.

ELSA (*twirling round on first stone*)
Ding-dong, Castle Bell!
(*waving to Elsinore*)
Farewell to my brother!
Ding-dong, Castle Bell!

(waving into distance)
Farewell to my mother!
(pointing to Elsinore)
You're scared, Elsinore! You're always scared!

CHILDREN (*dancing round Elsinore and chanting*)
Elsinore's a scaredy-cat,
A scaredy-cat, a scaredy-cat,
Elsinore's a scaredy-cat.
Daren't go near the castle!

ELSINORE Leave me alone. (*He backs away from the group.*)

AVA They do say that old mother Cat-Owl is really a witch.

ELSA I don't believe in witches.

HILD They say that a person can't move if he goes within a hundred steps of the castle walls.

GART That's right! He's turned into a statue.

ELSA You don't believe all that, do you?

BOYS Mmm, well...

MENNI I do! My mother told me never to go near the castle because old mother Cat-Owl will come out and catch me.

ELSA What if Cat-Owl does catch you?

MENNI She'll change me into a bird. Then she'll shut me up in a wicker-work basket and hang me up on the castle wall.

HILD (*fearfully*) They do say that there are thousands of birds in the castle. And every night old mother Cat-Owl goes out hunting for more victims.

ELSA Then why is she called CAT-Owl?

GART Because...because...(*in loud whisper*) because when morning comes, she changes into a CAT!

ELSA What rubbish! I don't believe a word of it.

ELSINORE	(*coming back to group*) You will if you get caught, Elsa. One day Cat-Owl may catch you and change you into...
ELSA	...an eagle! I'll change into a great eagle and fly up to the top of the highest mountain. (*She waves her arms.*)
AVA	I'll be a kingfisher.
HILD	And I'll be a stork, (*She stands on one leg.*)...and sit on people's roof tops.
GART	I'll be a goose! (*He flaps his arms.*)
MENNI	And I'll be a swan. (*He spreads his arms.*)
ELSINORE	I'll be...er...
ELSA	You'll be a frightened little sparrow, Elsinore! (*moving towards him making witch-like movements*) And wicked old Cat-Owl will come and GET YOU...first!
AVA	Do you believe in witches, Elsinore?
ELSINORE	No, I don't.
HILD	I wonder...I know! Let's play TRUTH OR DARE, everybody.
CHILDREN	Yes! Yes!
GART	Begin with Elsinore.
MENNI	We'll ask Elsinore first. TRUTH OR DARE, Elsinore?
ELSA	He's sure to say TRUTH, because he doesn't ever DARE anything! Ask him if he believes in witches, because I know he does!
ELSINORE	I'm not having TRUTH...I'm having...DARE.
CHILDREN	(surprised) DARE! Elsinore!
AVA	All right, Elsinore. We dare you to walk on Cat-Owl's stones...to the castle wall and bring back...an ivy leaf.

ELSA	(*clapping hands*) The two-coloured kind! That's the only place where the two-coloured kind grows. My mother said so.
AVA	Go on, Elsinore, or we shall write COWARD on a piece of card and hang it round your neck.
	(CHILDREN *laugh and then look silently at Elsinore.*)
ELSINORE	(*desperately*) All right! All right! (*taking a big breath*) I'll go. (*He goes out.*)
AVA	I didn't think he'd dare to go.
HILD	Nor did I. Perhaps...we tease him too much.
ELSA	He won't go to the castle. I know Elsinore too well. He'll just go home another way. (*A faint cry is heard.*)
GART	What was that?
ELSA	(*teasingly*) CAT-OWL'S COMING TO GET US!
MENNI	Come on! It's time to go home.
CHILDREN	Let's go! Come on!
	(ALL *run out, except* ELSA, *who lingers behind.*)
ELSA	I'd like to see old mother Cat-Owl get ME! (*She laughs.*) I'd show her! I know! I'll give her a call. (*calls loudly*) CAT-OWL! CAT-OWW-LL!
	(MAG *appears on the stones.*)
MAG	Caw-caw! (*flapping wings excitedly*) It's a little brown girl. (*calls softly*) Bel! Bel!
ELSA	(*with back to Mag*) I'll call again. CAT-OWL! CAT-OWW-LL!
	(BEL *hops in and inspects Elsa.*)
BEL	A bold little bird indeed. Call Mistress, Mag! Call Mistress!
MAG	(*softly*) Caw-caw! (*goes back along stones*) Caw-caw! (*loudly*) CAW-CAW!

53

ELSA   *(turning round)* Oh! It's only a rabbit. Come here, rabbit! *(She tries to catch* BEL, *who hops onto a stone.)* Come here!

BEL   *(hopping angrily onto next stone)* Rabbit! Look at the length of my ears, girl. Look at my ears.

ELSA   *(standing on a stone)* Come here! *(laughing)* Let me stroke your ears, rabbit!

BEL   *(hopping round Elsa)*
LEP–US TIMID–US,
you little IG–NOR–AM–US!

ELSA   What ARE you talking about?

BEL   LEP–US TIMID–US. I am HARE...Lepus Timidus, you ignorant child.

*(*CAT-OWL *appears, followed by* MAG *and* RAGGY-LIDDY, *who is carrying a silver cord.)*

CAT-OWL   *(softly)* Raggy! *(points to Elsa)* Atter-er, catcher-er!

*(*RAGGY-LIDDY *runs forward and slips cord round Elsa's ankle.)*

ELSA   *(turning and seeing Cat-Owl)* Oh! Who are you? You're not...?

CAT-OWL   Atter-er, catcher-er,
Whoo-shoo-hoo!
Atter-er, catcher-er,
Whoo-whoo-whoooo!

*(*RAGGY-LIDDY *gives end of cord to Cat-Owl.)*

ELSA   *(scornfully)* What a lot of rubbish! I'm not scared of you, Cat-Owl! You're just...OW! *(She screams as* CAT-OWL *jerks cord tightly round her ankle.)* OW! OWW!

CAT-OWL   Got you, my little bird! Now...what kind of little bird have we caught today, Bel?

BEL   An IGNORAMUS bird, Mistress! A little KNOW-NOTHING!

ELSA	You're hurting my ankle with this cord. (*to Raggy-Liddy*) Loosen it a little please!
RAGGY-LIDDY	(*bending down*) Poor thing! Let me...just a little...
CAT-OWL	Poor thing, indeed! (*flicking Raggy-Liddy with end of the cord*) Leave the little bird alone, Raggy. (*jerking cord*) Little birds must learn to suffer a little.
ELSA	Oh! Oh! (*beginning to sob quietly*) I'm not a bird. You know I'm not a bird. I'm Elsa...I'm...
BEL	Elsa, the IGNORAMUS bird! But you'll like her, Mistress. She's a bold one.
MAG	She's not bold now! Caw-caw! Look at her!
RAGGY-LIDDY	Poor thing! Poor thing!
CAT-OWL	(*flicking Raggy-Liddy with the cord*) Stop whining, Raggy! (*looking closely at Elsa*) A brown bird... ah-ha! (*cackling*)...yes...a brown bird.
BEL	Can I have her, Mistress? I like her.
MAG	I found her, Mistress. Give her to ME.
CAT-OWL	(*angrily*) No! Not likely! Here! (*giving cord to Raggy-Liddy*) Take her to the castle and shut her in a cage until I come.

(RAGGY-LIDDY *goes out pulling* ELSA *along behind her.*)

Come here, Bel! Come here, Mag!

BEL, MAG	(*hopping forward*) Yes, Mistress?
CAT-OWL	(*flicking at them*) They're all mine! Do you hear? All the birds are MINE. (*She shoos Bel and Mag.*) Now... hie away, to my Castle grey. Hie away!

(BEL *and* MAG *scurry out and* CAT-OWL *runs onto first stone and raises arms.*)

CAT-OWL *cont.* On grey stone one,
is trouble done!
He who stands here
will suffer dear. (*She runs onto second and then third stones.*)
Stones two and three,
work for me!
Hear my word,
CATCH A BIRD! (*She creeps out muttering.*)

(JORINDA *and* JORINDEL *come in.*)

JORINDA Look! Stones! They must lead somewhere. I'm going to walk on them.

JORINDEL (*pulling* JORINDA *back*) Wait! Stones like these can lead to...DANGER!

JORINDA (*surprised*) Why do you say that? (*walking towards stones and staring at them*) They are quite ordinary stones.

JORINDEL I don't know what it is, but I don't like this place. Come, Jorinda, we must find our way home now.

JORINDA Let me see if these stones lead anywhere, first. (*She runs along stones and stands still on third one.*)

JORINDEL Come back! Jorinda!

JORINDA (*standing quite still*) I can't...can't...can't...(*Her voice trails away and she hangs her head.*)
I'm...I'm...
I'm...a little bird,
With a necklace red,
Sing sorrow, sorrow, sorrow.
The little bird
May soon be dead,
'Ere 'morrow, 'morrow, 'morrow.

JORINDEL   (*running onto first stone and stretching out hands towards her*) I can't...can't...can't...(*His voice trails away.*) I'm turned to stone, stone, stone.

(CAT-OWL *creeps in.*)

CAT-OWL   Ah-ha! Ah-ha! (*rubbing hands together gleefully*) Alone, alone, alone, ha-hee!
The stones have done their work for me!
(*calls*) RAGGY! (*She inspects Jorinda.*) What a lovely little creature! (*cackling*) How sensible of you to wear your red necklace. It will make a pretty ruff of feathers for you, my dear. (*She cackles.*)

JORINDA   I'm a little bird,
With a necklace red...

(RAGGY-LIDDY *appears carrying a silver cord.*)

RAGGY-LIDDY   You called, Mistress?

CAT-OWL   Atter-er, catcher-er! (RAGGY-LIDDY *runs forward and slips cord round Jorinda's ankle.*)
Take her home, Raggy.
Hie away,
to my Castle grey.
Hie away!

(RAGGY-LIDDY *pulls* JORINDA *out.*)

JORINDEL   Do not take Jorinda away from me.

CAT-OWL   (*cackling*) The charm is around her,
                    the spell has bound her.

JORINDEL   Please give her back to me.

CAT-OWL   (*cackling*) I have her fast.
                    Her doom is cast.

JORINDEL   (*in despair*) No! No!

CAT-OWL (*fixing eyes on Jorindel and raising arms over first stone*)
My work's now done
on grey stone one.
So shall it be
that you go free.
Hie away, boy! Hie away!
(*She goes out cackling as* JORINDEL *moves slowly off stone.*)

JORINDEL My Jorinda is gone.
What shall I do?
O sorrow, sorrow, sorrow!

EGG-WIFE JUST SUPPOSE that...you were Jorindel, (*She looks round at the listeners.*) in that evil place. Wouldn't *you* have felt lonely, sad and afraid? Poor Jorindel wandered for a long time, searching for his Jorinda. Then...over the hill, where the trees meet the sky, (*pointing*) darkness fell! And Jorindel sank into a troubled sleep.

(FAIRY QUEEN *runs into arena, followed by* FLOWER FAIRIES.)

FAIRY QUEEN Follow, follow, follow me,
All fairy flowers that be.

FAIRIES Hand in hand we'll dance around (*They dance.*)
And make this place ENCHANTED GROUND!

PEARL (*pointing to Jorindel*) Fairy Queen! What have we here?

FAIRY QUEEN (*looking at Jorindel*) A victim of Cat-Owl, I fear.

FAIRIES (*trilling*) Cat-O-w-l...Cat-Ow-w-l...Cat-Ow-w-l.

FAIRY QUEEN Cat-Owl has done this boy some harm,
So we must make a fairy charm.

FAIRIES (*trilling*) Charm-m-m...charm-m-m...charm-m-m.
(*They form a semi-circle round Jorindel.*)

YELLOW FAIRIES	We will weave a magic spell Of buttercup and cowslip bell.
BLUE FAIRIES	Forget-me-not and speedwell blue, Here we give you petals...two.
RED FAIRIES	Fragrant rose and poppy red From a fairy garden bed.
PEARL	A drop of dew, a grain of sand, Gathered by a fairy's hand.
FAIRY QUEEN	(*placing a red flower with a pearl-like centre in Jorindel's hand*) Now our magic is complete, So dance around on fairy feet. (*They dance.*)
FAIRIES	Hand in hand we dance around And make this place ENCHANTED GROUND.
FAIRY QUEEN	Away, away Never stay, All be gone, 'Tis break of day. (*All* FAIRIES *dance out.*)
EGG-WIFE	Now...JUST SUPPOSE that...as the sun came up over the hill (*pointing*) where the trees meet the sky, Jorindel awoke...and found...the MAGIC FLOWER! (*She leans forward to listeners.*) You saw the Fairy Queen put it in his hand, didn't you? (JORINDEL *gradually wakes and looks round.*)
JORINDEL	Yes, they were all here...the Flower Fairies and their Queen. And now this flower is in my hand. I wonder...(*looking closely at flower*) Ah! There is a dew-drop in the middle just like a pearl. I wonder... (MAG *appears on stones.*)
MAG	(*softly*) Caw-caw! Another one! Another one!
JORINDEL	(*jumping up*) No, it's not! Go away, you old villain. (*He hides the flower under his cloak.*)

MAG	(*flapping wings excitedly and running round Jorindel*) What's that you've got?
JORINDEL	Nothing! (*hitting out at Mag*) Get away! Get back to your wicked old witch. Go on!
MAG	Caw-caw! You've got something. Mag wants it. Give! Give!
JORINDEL	No!
MAG	Give! Give! (*He pecks at Jorindel's hands.*)
JORINDEL	(*holding cloak tightly*) No!
	(MAG *chases* JORINDEL *round arena as* BEL *appears on stones.*)
BEL	Leave! Leave!
MAG	(*flapping excitedly*) Boy has a secret. Boy is hiding his secret. Get! Get!
BEL	(*to Mag*) Bel will make Boy give up his secret, Mag. (*cunningly to Jorindel*) Give Bel your secret, Boy, and Bel will tell you of your birdie's fate.
JORINDEL	Fate! What do you mean?
BEL	Your birdie with the red, red ring, Cries, 'Sorrow, sorrow, sorrow.' It sings the end of everything, Oh sorrow, sorrow, sorrow!
JORINDEL	(*terrified*) The end of everything! What do you mean? Tell me what has happened to my Jorinda.
BEL	Give Bel your secret, Boy, the one you are hiding there under your cloak.
JORINDEL	No!
MAG	Caw-caw! Fetch Mistress! (*He begins to flap away over the stones.*)
BEL	No, Mag! (*stroking ears*) Bel will think.
MAG	Caw-caw! (*flapping back to Bel*) What can you do?

(BEL *whispers to* MAG *who nods.*)

BEL   (*aloud*) Bel has long ears. (*hopping up to Jorindel*) Bel will find a way.

JORINDEL   (*angrily*) What do I care for your long ears? (*He hits out at Bel who sees the red flower.*)

BEL   (*screaming in terror*) Aw-w! Aw-w!

MAG   Caw-caw! Caw-CAW!

BEL   He has the...(*putting fore-paws over mouth*) Come away, Mag! Hie away! (*They run off.*)

JORINDEL   (*looking at flower*) So there IS something very special about this flower.

(RAGGY-LIDDY *appears on stones.*)

Oh! It's only the poor servant girl. She won't harm me. What do you want, girl?

RAGGY-LIDDY   (*coming closer*) What's that you've got in your hand?

JORINDEL   (*putting flower under cloak*) Nothing to do with you, girl. What do you want with me, anyway?

RAGGY-LIDDY   I came to tell you about the little bird.

JORINDEL   (*eagerly*) What little bird? Tell me, is my dear Jorinda safe and well?

RAGGY-LIDDY   (*sadly*) There is only a little red bird now.

JORINDEL   What do you mean? Jorinda is a girl, not a little bird.

RAGGY-LIDDY   Once Cat-Owl's birds were all girls. Now they are birds.

JORINDEL   But how? How can girls change into birds? It's not possible.

RAGGY-LIDDY   Mistress makes magic spells.

JORINDEL   How?

RAGGY-LIDDY	(*holding up arms and miming*)
	Foot to claw,
	Hand to wing,
	Nose to beak,
	Sing, bird sing!
	They are all very pretty birds, not like poor Raggy.
	Raggy's not a pretty bird. (*She hangs her head.*)
JORINDEL	I don't understand what you mean. What are you trying to tell me? Come here!
RAGGY-LIDDY	(*fearfully*) No! No! (*She moves towards stones.*) Raggy is only Cat-Owl's servant. Raggy never tells!
JORINDEL	Don't go!
RAGGY-LIDDY	Raggy must go now. Mistress may call.
JORINDEL	(*putting out hand*) Wait! Tell me...
RAGGY-LIDDY	No! Raggy never tells anything!
	(*loudly*) Raggy's not a pretty bird,
	So Raggy is a servant girl.
	(*She puts her hand over her mouth and runs out.*)
JORINDEL	She WAS trying to tell me something. (*Noises are heard.*) What's that? Someone's coming! I'll hide behind this bush. (*He moves to side.*)
	(MAG *and* BEL *appear, holding a long cord. They jerk it a few times, then pull* ELSA *into the arena, wearing a bird mask.*)
MAG	Caw-caw! (*flapping wings*) Mistress will roast us! Mistress will kill us!
BEL	Mistress will have to catch us first.
MAG	Mistress can catch anything, Bel. She'll catch us. I know she will.
BEL	She won't catch me, or my little brown bird.
MAG	The brown bird is mine, too. I found her.

BEL Mistress doesn't like her, anyway. Mistress doesn't like little brown birds. (*scratching Elsa's head*) But I like you, little bird, even though you are so plain. (*to Mag*) But I liked her better when she could talk.

MAG Make her sing, Bel.

BEL I've tried, but she shakes her head. Look!

MAG I'll try. (*scratching Elsa's head*) Caw-caw! Caw-caw!

(ELSA *pecks angrily at Mag.*)

Ugh! She's a nasty little thing.

BEL I know she is, but I like her. Listen! (*cocking ear*) Someone's coming.

(RAGGY-LIDDY *appears from right.*)

MAG What do you want, Raggy?

RAGGY-LIDDY I saw you! I saw you! What are you doing with Mistress's bird?

BEL Mag and I have decided to leave the castle, Raggy.

RAGGY-LIDDY (*quickly*) Take me! Take me!

MAG Caw-caw! We don't want you, Raggy.

BEL Don't be foolish, Mag. We shall need a servant.

(*As they talk,* CAT-OWL *comes in from left.*)

CAT-OWL (*screaming*) Whoo! Whoo! What are you doing with my bird? You've stolen one of my birds. I'll roast you...I'll kill you...Come here, Mag.

MAG (*in terror*) Caw-caw! I told you she would catch us, Bel.

(BEL *covers ears with hands.*)

CAT-OWL (*furiously*) You've stolen one of my birds. It's that brown one you wanted, Bel. Come HERE!

BEL	I'm warning you, Mistress. You're going to lose your power.
CAT-OWL	(*screeching*) You're a liar, Bel! I'll kill you for this.
BEL	(*dodging away*) You're going to lose your power. And I'll tell you how...(*All stand quite still for a moment.*) The boy who was with the little red bird has found THE MAGIC FLOWER.
CAT-OWL	(*angrily*) How do you know? You're just making it up.
BEL	He has it under his cloak. I saw it, I tell you.
CAT-OWL	You're a liar, Bel. You were always a liar. I don't believe you.

(JORINDEL *steps from hiding place, holding red flower in front of him.*)

JORINDEL	(*loudly*) Then turn your evil eyes this way and see for yourself.
CAT-OWL	(*screams*) Black spirits and white, Red spirits and grey, Mingle! Mingle! Mingle! CURSE THIS EVIL DAY!

(RAGGY-LIDDY *creeps out quietly.*)

JORINDEL	Your curses will do you no good now, Cat-Owl. (*pointing flower at her*) Oh, magic flower, Destroy her power!
CAT-OWL	(*screams*) Ah-h-h-h-h! (*She creeps away to side of arena.*)
JORINDEL	(*pointing flower at Bel and Mag*) No more evil do!
BEL, MAG	Ah-h-h-h-h! (*They creep to side of arena.*)
JORINDEL	(*to Elsa*) Come here, little bird. (*touching her with flower*)

A drop of dew,
A grain of sand,
Claw to foot,
Wing to hand!

(ELSA *pulls back bird mask with hands.*)

ELSA　I'm free! I'm free!

JORINDEL　Now take me to Jorinda.

(*As he speaks,* RAGGY-LIDDY *appears with* JORINDA *in bird mask, on silver cord.*)

RAGGY-LIDDY　She's here! Your little red bird is here.

(JORINDEL *runs to Jorinda.*)

JORINDEL　Jorinda! (*touching her with flower*)
A drop of dew,
A grain of sand,
Claw to foot,
Wing to hand!

(JORINDA *pulls back bird mask with hands.*)

Oh! At last I have you back, my dear Jorinda.

JORINDA　I was beginning to despair. I was beginning to think I would never see you again. (*taking his hand*) How happy I am.

JORINDEL　Now we are both happy again.

RAGGY-LIDDY　(*sadly*) What about me?

JORINDEL　You?

JORINDA　(*putting arms round Raggy-Liddy*) Poor Raggy! (*to Jorindel*) She tried to be kind to me. What can we do for her?

RAGGY-LIDDY　Cat-Owl had me in her magic power,
So touch me with your magic flower!

(*As* JORINDEL *touches Raggy-Liddy, the* FLOWER FAIRIES *run in and put a flowered head-dress on her head.*)

RAGGY-LIDDY   (*touching head-dress of wild flowers*)
Ear of corn and leaf of clover,
Now the wicked charm is over! (*to Jorindel*)
Come boy! We must go to the castle and set all
the birds free.

ELSA   Free! Free! All must be free! (*She runs up the
stones towards the castle.*)

JORINDA   (*following*) All must be free!

JORINDEL   (*turning to Cat-Owl, Bel and Mag*)
Get you hence! You have no power,
For I have THE MAGIC FLOWER!
(*They creep out as* JORINDEL *runs off after the
others towards castle.*)

ALL FAIRIES   And hand in hand we'll dance around,
And make the castle...FAIRY GROUND!
(*They all dance out.*)

END OF THIRD PLAY

PLAYWATCHERS

People of Cassel

EGG-WIFE (*sitting back contentedly*) There! My tale is done!

LISTENERS (*clapping*) Another one! Another one!

EGG-WIFE (*getting up*) Another day! (*tapping head*) My tales are safe in here. (*She goes out.*)

JACOB How well she told her story.

LISTENERS She did! She did! (*They stand in groups 'talking' about the story.*)

WILHELM (*to Jacob*) A tale, well told, is treasure, brother.

(JACOB *and* WILHELM *walk back to bench.*)

JACOB Treasure indeed! And it must never be lost. We'll search and search, then make one great book of all these tales.

WILHELM And each tale we find will be...like a forgotten ear of corn lying in some sheltered corner...

JACOB Go on, brother!

WILHELM ...then, when the sun begins to shine again, it will grow – and be more precious than the rest – to those who find it.

JACOB (*banging pile of notebooks*) It must be done!

WILHELM (*excitedly*) What shall we call the book, Jacob?

JACOB Nothing fanciful, I think. These tales come from the hearths and homes of country folk.

WILHELM   Then they'll be...household tales. (*He turns pages of the notebook.*) The Turnip...The Three Sons of Fortune...The Valiant Little Tailor...

JACOB   And now, today, The Proud Princess...

(*The Proud Princess* PLAYMAKERS *come in and bow, to applause.*)

Straw into Gold...

(*Straw into Gold* PLAYMAKERS *come in and bow, to applause.*)

The Castle of Birds...

(*The Castle of Birds* PLAYMAKERS *come in and bow, to applause.*)

WILHELM   Brother! It's as I said. They're HOUSEHOLD TALES!

JACOB   That's it! We'll call our treasure...'Household tales'.

LISTENERS   (*applauding*) HOUSEHOLD TALES! HOUSEHOLD TALES! (*They all go out repeating,* 'Household tales'.)

Minstrels' Song

Music: Traditional American

We're a mer - ry band of min-strels march - ing

free,_____ We're a mer - ry band of

min - strels full of glee,_____ We're a

mer - ry band of min-strels, Mer - ry band of

min - strels, A mer - ry band of

min - strels march - ing free._____

Suggestions for the Playmakers

If you are one of
the Brothers Grimm
you can dress
like this.

The Old Soldier
can dress like
this.

The Artist can
dress like this.

The Egg-Wife can
dress like
this.

You can make all kinds of masks.

You can make half-masks for the kelpies. These are comfortable to wear and leave your mouth free for talking.

First make a paper pattern by folding a thin piece of paper in half.
Hold the paper over your face and mark your eye and nose spots with a pencil. (Be careful not to poke the pencil through!)

Cut the eye and nose holes, then cut the rest of the mask shape. Test it to see that it fits.

Pin your paper pattern onto a piece of hessian and cut it out. Then sew it onto a woolly hat.

Make a long mask of hessian, sewn onto an old woolly hat for Rumplestiltskin.
Cut out large eye, nose and mouth holes. Use raffia or thick wool to make the face very hairy.

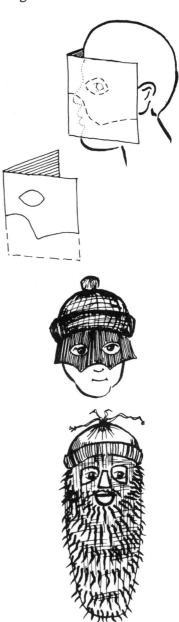

Make bird masks, which can be pushed back easily, like this.

Fold a piece of thin card in half. Mark your eye spot and cut out a nose hole.
Cut out eye holes. Draw and then cut out feather shapes.
Tape or staple a beak into the nose hole. Decorate the eyes.
Attach a loop of elastic to hold the mask in place.

beak

Make a hat for Cat-Owl like this.
Cut out a quarter circle with radius 40 cm.
Glue it into a cone.
Cut a circle with radius 18 cm. Cut out a circle with radius 7 cm from the middle.
Snip the inside edges of the ring.
Slip the ring over the cone.
Stick the cone to the brim under the snips.

Make a mask for Bel, the hare, like this.

Cat-Owl and Raggy-Liddy can wear costumes made from old dresses.
Sew old coloured stockings and tights onto the dress.

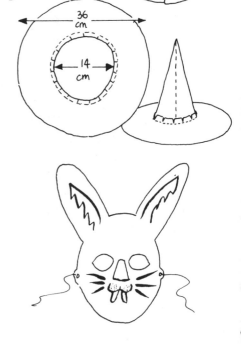